D0191047

Teacher's Pet

Other Apple Books
by JOHANNA HURWITZ

Teacher's Pet

JOHANNA HURWITZ

Illustrations by SHEILA HAMANAKA

A
LITTLE APPLE
PAPERBACK

SCHOLASTIC INC.

New York   Toronto   London   Auckland   Sydney

No part of this publication may be reproduced in whole or in part, or stored in a retrieval system, or transmitted in any form or by any means, electronic, mechanical, photocopying, recording, or otherwise, without written permission of the publisher. For information regarding permission, write to William Morrow and Company, Inc., 105 Madison Avenue, New York, NY 10016.

ISBN 0-590-42031-3

Text copyright © 1988 by Johanna Hurwitz.
Illustrations copyright © 1988 by Sheila Hamanaka.
All rights reserved. Published by Scholastic Inc.,
730 Broadway, New York, NY 10003, by arrangement with
William Morrow and Company, Inc.

APPLE PAPERBACKS is a registered trademark of Scholastic Inc.

12 11 10 9   4/9

Printed in the U.S.A.   40

First Scholastic printing, September 1989

For my friend
Marilyn Freilicher Brownstein,
in a class by herself

Contents

Teacher's Pet

1

The
Pickle
Club

It was the first day of school.

Cricket Kaufman liked to plan ahead. For three weeks she had known what she would wear to school today. And she had bought all her school supplies over a week ago. Cricket loved buying a new notebook and new crayons and new pencils. Everything felt clean and smooth to her touch. At home, she had even enjoyed *smelling* the new notebook. But of course she wouldn't do a thing like that sitting here at her desk. The other kids in her fourth-grade class would think she was weird.

Cricket loved school. She loved her teachers. And every year since she had been in kindergarten, her teachers had loved her. It was no wonder. No student was more perfect than Cricket Kaufman. She was a dependable and helpful student who always paid attention and behaved like an angel. Her papers were always neat and her homework was always completed. She wasn't like those goof-offs Lucas Cott and his sidekick Julio Sanchez who were sitting in the back row. Cricket knew it would only take a short while until Mrs. Schraalenburgh, her new teacher, realized how lucky she was to have Cricket in her class! All of the teachers who had ever had Cricket in their classes had called her *a joy*. She was always the teacher's pet.

Cricket looked around to see who else was in Mrs. Schraalenburgh's class. She recognized everyone because even if they hadn't been in third grade with her last year, they had been in her second-grade class the year before that. There were three sections of each grade and each year the children were moved from one section to another. When Cricket was in the first and second grades, Mary Claire Shea had been in classes with Cricket and had been her best friend.

But Mary Claire had moved away during the summer after second grade and Cricket had been without a best friend all during third grade. But that year, Cricket's sister Monica had been born. Someday, Monica would be big enough to be a friend, and then it wouldn't matter anymore if Cricket had a special friend at school or not.

As she sat waiting for school to begin, Cricket quietly turned the ring on her finger around and around. The ring had been a special gift from her parents when Monica was born. Cricket had wanted a ring for as long as she could remember. But her mother had always said that if she had one, she would probably lose it. Mrs. Kaufman presented Cricket with a tiny box on the day that Monica came home from the hospital. Inside was a silver ring with a dark red stone. "It's your birthstone," her mother explained. "It's a garnet because you were born in January."

The ring fit perfectly on the middle finger of Cricket's right hand.

"Whatever you do, don't take your ring off," Mrs. Kaufman had warned her daughter. "That's the best way to lose it."

Cricket certainly did not want to lose her

new ring. She was very proud of it. So although she sometimes took the ring off at home, she was very careful never to take it off at school. But often, when she was sitting quietly at her desk, she turned it around and around on her finger.

Mrs. Schraalenburgh entered the room. She was very tall and had curly white hair. Cricket had heard that she was really strict, but Cricket wasn't afraid of her. Cricket was such a good student that she even got along with the strictest teachers who gave the most homework. Cricket liked doing her homework. It kept her busy on the afternoons when she didn't have piano lessons.

Behind Mrs. Schraalenburgh came a girl that Cricket had never seen before. She must be a new student in the school, Cricket thought. Cricket wondered if this girl was as smart as she was. She doubted it. She had always been the smartest person in her class.

The new girl sat in a front seat right across from Cricket. Cricket liked sitting in front because that way she had a better chance of being chosen as a monitor to deliver messages or run errands for her teacher. Sometimes teachers seated the students according to size. Other teachers used alphabetical order. But Mrs. Schraalenburgh told them that they could sit wherever they wished for the first week. Of course, Lucas and Julio took seats in the last row. Cricket had known they would do that.

Before Mrs. Schraalenburgh began to call the roll, she said, "I know many of you from seeing you around the building when you were younger. And some of you have older siblings who were in my class in the past."

"Siblings?" Julio called out. "What's that?"

"Who knows what . . ."

Cricket's hand was waving in the air.

"I haven't even finished my question," said Mrs. Schraalenburgh. "Why are you raising your hand?"

"Because I know the answer," said Cricket.

"She always knows the answers," said a voice from the back. That was Lucas Cott speaking.

Cricket smiled at this recognition from her classmate. She wanted to be a lawyer when she grew up, and always knowing the answer and reacting quickly were important to her.

"Very well," said Mrs. Schraalenburgh. "What is my question and what is the answer?"

"You were going to ask what a sibling is," said Cricket. "And the answer is that it's a brother or a sister."

"You are absolutely correct," said the teacher. She smiled at Cricket and Cricket smiled back at her. There, she thought to herself, I've only been in fourth grade for five minutes, but Mrs. Schraalenburgh already knows how smart I am.

The teacher began calling the names of the students.

"Connie Alf."

"Here," called Connie, waving her hand.

"Lisa Benson."

"Here," Lisa called out.

"Hope Dubbin."

Name by name, Mrs. Schraalenburgh called the roll.

"Cricket Kaufman."

"Present," Cricket called out. She always said "present" instead of "here." It sounded more grown up.

"I wouldn't give her a present," a voice called out.

"Who said that?" asked Mrs. Schraalenburgh, standing up and looking around.

Cricket's face turned red. She knew who said it. She also knew that Mrs. Schraalenburgh couldn't recognize the voices of the fourth-graders yet.

"That was Julio," said Cricket. She hoped he would get into a lot of trouble now.

"We don't want tattletales in our class," said Mrs. Schraalenburgh sharply. She looked at Cricket. "But we do want good manners and polite behavior. I do not want to hear any of you speaking out unless I call on you first. Is that understood?"

"Yes, Mrs. Schraalenburgh" said some of the students.

Cricket felt awful. The teacher had asked who had spoken and when Julio wouldn't admit to it, Cricket had told on him. It was bad enough that he said something nasty about her. But instead of scolding Julio, Mrs. Schraalenburgh had made it seem as if Cricket had done something wrong. It wasn't fair.

"Zoe Mitchell," said the teacher returning to the roll call.

"Here," said a voice across the aisle from Cricket.

"Zoe, please stand up a moment so that

everyone can see who you are," said Mrs. Schraalenburgh. "Zoe has just moved to town and is new to our school. We're delighted that you were able to make it for the first day," said the teacher. "Since you are new, why don't you tell the rest of the class something about yourself?"

Zoe stood up. Instead of looking around shyly the way most of the kids would have if they had been asked to speak, she smiled and started talking. "My mother and my older sister Halley, who is in sixth grade, and I just moved here because my mother remarried. Now I have a new stepfather and stepgrandparents and we live in a new house. And I have my own room, too," she added.

"Excellent," said Mrs. Schraalenburgh, smiling at Zoe. "Welcome to our school and our town. We're happy to have you here."

Cricket looked across at her new classmate as she sat down. She wasn't sure *she* was so happy to have her here. She sounded too stuck up.

When roll call was completed, Mrs. Schraalenburgh had many announcements to make. One of the things she said was that this year the school was planning to collect soup-can labels. When enough labels were sent to the company that had made the soup, the school would be given audio-visual equipment. With a lot of soup labels, the school might have a new film-strip machine or cassette player.

"A good thing to do would be to ask your friends and relatives to start saving these labels, too," said Mrs. Schraalenburgh. "That way we'll get even more." Cricket made a mental note to ask her mother to serve more soup to the family.

After the announcements, Mrs. Schraalenburgh picked several of the boys to help her pass out the textbooks. Lugging the books around was not something that Cricket cared about. But Zoe leaned over and whispered to her, "That's very sexist of her. Girls are strong enough to carry those books, too." Cricket had never thought of that.

Soon the morning was over and it was lunchtime. The lunchroom smells the same as last year, thought Cricket, as the students rushed in and took seats around the tables. Cricket put her lunch box down and hurried to the milk line. Today, because it was the first day of school, her mother had said that she could buy chocolate milk.

Back at the table, Cricket discovered that

she was sitting next to Zoe. "Look what I have,"
said the new girl, unwrapping a piece of alumi-
num foil. Inside the foil was a huge pickle.

"Lucky you," called out Hope.

"Do you want a bite?" Zoe offered. She
passed the pickle down toward Hope.

Cricket wrinkled her nose. She didn't like
pickles. She couldn't even stand the smell of
them.

"Can I have a bite, too?" asked Lisa.

"Sure," said Zoe. "It's big enough so that
everyone can have some."

"You'll get germs if you let so many people
take bites out of your pickle," said Cricket.

"It's worth the risk," said Hope, crunching down on her mouthful of pickle. "It's wonderful."

"Hmmm," Lisa agreed.

The pickle was passed from hand to hand around the table. Everyone took a nibble of it. When it reached Cricket, she passed it on to Zoe.

"Don't you want any?" asked Zoe. "Are you afraid of all our germs?"

"I don't like pickles," Cricket admitted. She wiped the hand that had touched the pickle on her napkin. She hoped she wouldn't smell like a pickle for the rest of the afternoon.

"You don't know what you are missing. This is wonderful," said Zoe, taking a bite. "When was the last time you tasted a pickle?"

Cricket shrugged her shoulders. She couldn't remember. Maybe she had never tasted a pickle. She just knew she didn't like them.

"Come on," urged Zoe, handing the pickle back to Cricket. "Take a tiny bite. I'll bet you love it."

"It was delicious," said Hope. "I'm going to ask my mother to put a pickle in my lunch tomorrow."

"Me too," said Lisa.

"We could have a pickle club and every day somebody else could bring a pickle for lunch," suggested Zoe.

"That's a great idea," said Hope, licking her fingers.

Cricket took the pickle from Zoe. She didn't want to be left out. Maybe if she took just a very small bite of the pickle it wouldn't be too bad. She put it to her mouth and took the tiniest bite possible. The shred of sour pickle landed on her tongue. It tasted worse than it smelled. It was horrible. Cricket felt her eyes roll back in her head as she gagged into her napkin.

"I guess you can't be in the pickle club," said Zoe, taking back her pickle.

Cricket took a long drink of her chocolate milk through the straw. But the sour taste remained in her mouth. Who'd want to be in a pickle club? she thought to herself. It was the stupidest thing that she had ever heard of.

All during the rest of the lunch period, Cricket was in a bad mood. She had been looking forward to school so much and now that it had begun, things weren't going at all the way she had imagined them. She turned her ring around and around on her finger and thought about the morning.

Zoe was talking with the other girls at the table as if she had known them all her life. Cricket looked at Zoe and wondered why she had been put into Mrs. Schraalenburgh's section of fourth grade. Why couldn't she have been assigned to one of the other classes? She blamed Zoe for both the bad taste in her mouth and the bad feeling that she had. Even if all the other girls seemed to like her, Cricket did not like the new girl at all.

2

Hiccups

Back in the classroom, Mrs. Schraalenburgh began to tell the class about a book that she was going to read aloud to them. It was *Mr. Popper's Penguins*. Cricket's hand flew up into the air.

"Yes, Cricket?" asked the teacher. "What do you want?"

"I already read that book by myself," Cricket announced proudly. She had read it during the summer vacation.

"You did?" Mrs. Schraalenburgh looked surprised. "Well, you must be a very good reader."

"I am," said Cricket.

"Good. Now, let's see if you can be a good listener, too," said the teacher.

A pencil rolled onto the floor from someone's desk.

"Take everything off your desks," Mrs. Schraalenburgh instructed her students. "I don't want anything to distract you. This is a time for listening and putting your imaginations to work. I don't want to hear a sound."

Cricket knew that this would be difficult for Lucas and Julio. At the end of third grade, Lucas had been trying harder, but he still forgot and did silly things. And as for Julio, he didn't try at all. If she were the teacher, she wouldn't let those two boys sit next to each other. Mrs. Schraalenburgh would probably figure it out herself in another day or so. Lucas plus Julio equaled trouble.

Cricket sat back in her seat. She loved listening to stories. The only problem was that teachers never read for a long enough time. They would read one chapter and leave you waiting eagerly for them to go on. Then they would say that if you were good, they would continue with the story the next day. Cricket could never wait.

She would rush to the public library and take out a copy of the same book that the teacher had begun. Then she would quickly finish it at home. Cricket enjoyed hearing a story, even when she knew what was going to happen next, and was always able to listen quietly.

"It was an afternoon in late September," Mrs. Schraalenburgh read. "In the pleasant little city of Stillwater, Mr. Popper, the house painter, was going home from work."

"Hey. We're getting our house painted right now. The painter came this morning, just when I was leaving for school," Lucas called out.

"Maybe the man in this story is the guy painting your house," suggested Julio.

"I doubt it," said Mrs. Schraalenburgh. "Now, I don't want to have to tell you this again. There is to be no talking during story time. If you want to say something, you are to save it for later when I have finished. Do you understand?" She looked around the room. Cricket nodded her head vigorously. She was glad that she had already read *Mr. Popper's Penguins*. It was a funny story.

Mrs. Schraalenburgh began again. "It was an afternoon in late September. In the pleasant little city of Stillwater, Mr. Popper, the house painter, was going home from work."

Cricket worried for a moment that Julio or Lucas would call out and say that she had already told them that. But luckily no one spoke. All was quiet in the classroom as the teacher continued reading. Suddenly Cricket hiccuped. She swallowed hard. She wondered why now, of all times, she had to start hiccuping. Her mouth hadn't been open, so she couldn't have swallowed any air.

"Hic!" A second little hiccup exploded inside her. Cricket felt her face turning red. Belching or having hiccups in the middle of story time was the sort of thing that one of the boys would do. It was not Cricket's way of behaving at all. When the third little hiccup came, she was waiting for it. She kept her lips firmly pressed together so she wouldn't make a sound. But she began to worry that she was going to hiccup all during the story. She waited tensely. A minute passed and nothing happened. Cricket gradually relaxed again. The hiccups have gone away as suddenly as they came, she thought. Then another one escaped from her throat. And because she hadn't been expecting it, it was the loudest one of all.

Mrs. Schraalenburgh looked up. She ges-

tured to Cricket to go outside and get a drink of water from the fountain in the hallway. Quietly, Cricket stood up and walked to the door. She was very embarrassed, especially when she made another loud hiccup before she could get outside.

She took a long drink of the lukewarm water at the fountain. It never tasted any good, but if it would stop her hiccups, she would be willing to drink a whole quart of it. She stood by the fountain, waiting. Nothing happened. The hic-

cups were really gone this time. Quietly, Cricket opened the door and tiptoed back into the classroom. She moved her chair quietly as she sat down. She knew that everyone was looking at her and thinking about her hiccups and not about Mr. Popper. And for a moment, she wished that she were in the Arctic or the Antarctic. Those were the places that Mr. Popper had always dreamed about going. Cricket had never wanted to go to the Arctic or Antarctic before, but right now she wanted to be anywhere but in her classroom. She didn't like being a nuisance in class. It was not the Cricket way of behaving.

Mrs. Schraalenburgh went on with her reading. Cricket sat back in her chair and concentrated hard on the story. "Hic!" Another hiccup popped out of her before she knew it.

A few kids began to giggle softly, but Mrs. Schraalenburgh acted as if she didn't hear. Cricket took deep breaths with her mouth closed. "Hic!" Another hiccup escaped. It was awful.

Cricket looked over at Zoe Mitchell. She was sitting still and looking straight ahead at the teacher. Cricket was certain that she was having hiccups because of the piece of pickle that Zoe had given her at lunchtime. It had to be the reason for her hiccups because she had never had them this way before. But why didn't Zoe have hiccups, too? And what about the other girls at the table who had taken bites out of the sour pickle?

"Hic!"

Cricket tried to hold her breath. She remembered having once heard that it was a way to stop hiccups. She looked at the clock above Mrs. Schraalenburgh's desk. She watched the second hand moving slowly around. If she could hold her breath for thirty seconds, perhaps the hiccups would finally disappear. The hand on the clock moved more slowly than usual. "*Hic!*" The loudest hiccup of all escaped from Cricket.

Mrs. Schraalenburgh put the book down. "You had better go to the nurse," she said to Cricket. "We can't have this sort of disturbance going on during story time."

Cricket got up from her desk again. This time she didn't take care to be quiet and her chair scraped against the wooden floor and made a noise.

"I can't help it," said Cricket. "I don't want to have hiccups. They just came." As she said it, she remembered the times in the past when Lucas or Julio or one of the other boys had developed a case of hiccups. That was what they always said. "I can't help it." She had never believed them. Now she was sure that Mrs. Schraalenburgh didn't believe her.

Cricket was afraid that she was going to start crying. That would be awful, hiccups and tears together. She rushed out of the room and heard the door bang behind her. Then she hurried down the hall to the nurse's office.

Mrs. Phillips, the nurse, was all alone. She was sorting papers when Cricket entered. "How are you, Cricket?" she asked. "You can't be sick. No one gets sick on the first day of school."

"I'm not sick," said Cricket as still another hiccup popped out. "But I've got hiccups and they won't go away."

"I once read about a man who had hiccups for two days," said Mrs. Phillips.

"You mean, I might have them that long?" asked Cricket anxiously.

"No, I know a secret cure for hiccups. The poor man who had them so long obviously didn't know it."

"What is it?" asked Cricket. She knew that some people said the best way to cure hiccups was to scare you. But she hated being scared. She looked around the nurse's office. Perhaps there was something that was going to jump out at her. Something that Mrs. Phillips had secretly rigged up to cure all the students in the school who ever came into her office with hiccups.

"Hic!" Another hiccup came from Cricket's throat. It was beginning to hurt, having so many hiccups.

"My mother used to put a paper bag over my head," said the nurse. She laughed.

Cricket wondered if that was what Mrs. Phillips was going to do to her. A paper bag wasn't scary.

"But I've discovered a better cure than that," continued the nurse. "You put a little sugar on your tongue and then you take a drink of water. It works like magic." She rummaged through a drawer in her desk. "I always keep a few of these handy," she said, taking out a little packet of sugar. It was the sort of packet that they have in restaurants for people who put sugar in their coffee.

"Stick out your tongue," said Mrs. Phillips.

Cricket obeyed the nurse. She felt the grains of sugar landing on her tongue. Then the nurse handed her a Styrofoam cup filled with water. Cricket took a long drink. Then she waited. Nothing happened.

"I think you're cured," said the nurse.

Cricket waited another minute to be on the safe side. When nothing happened at all, she smiled.

"They really are gone," she said.

"Just like magic," said the nurse. "The funny thing is that I have no idea why that trick works."

Cricket skipped down the hall to her classroom. When she got there, Mrs. Schraalenburgh was just putting the book away.

"My hiccups are all gone," Cricket announced.

"Good," said the teacher. "And I guess it's a good thing that you have already read *Mr. Popper's Penguins* because you missed so much of it."

"I'll hear the next part tomorrow," said Cricket. She was already planning that from now on, she would carry a little sugar packet in her pencil case. If hiccups happened once, they might happen again. Next time she would be prepared.

"I can't wait to get home and find out the name of the painter at my house," said Lucas when the bell rang for dismissal. Everyone charged out the door. Cricket was glad to be going home. Tomorrow was another day. Tomorrow she would have to work harder to make Mrs. Schraalenburgh realize how lucky she was to have Cricket in her class. She knew that today Mrs. Schraalenburgh had no idea of her good fortune.

3

Another Rotten Afternoon

"How was your first day of fourth grade?" Cricket's mother greeted her when she returned home after school. Usually, when she came in the house, Cricket bubbled over with stories about how many answers she knew and what good things the teacher had said about her. But today had been one big disappointment. So she just shrugged her shoulders.

"Do you have any homework?" asked Mrs. Kaufman.

"Not real homework," said Cricket. "There's nothing to write, but we're supposed to bring an old shirt or something to use for a smock in art class. And everyone is going to bring soup-can labels to school. Could we have soup for supper tonight?"

"I wasn't planning on soup for supper, but I have an idea," said Mrs. Kaufman, smiling. "I was going to make rice to go with our meal. I'll open a can of tomato soup and pour it on the rice and add some cheese. That way I won't have to change the menu and you can have the tomato-soup label."

Cricket beamed. She bet everyone else in her class forgot all about the labels. She would probably be the only one to bring one to school tomorrow. That would show Mrs. Schraalen-burgh how attentive she was and how good she was at remembering things!

The next morning, as soon as she was in her seat, Cricket raised her hand.

"Yes, Cricket?" called the teacher.

Cricket opened her notebook, which had a pocket made out of heavy paper inside the front cover. "I brought a soup label," she said.

"How nice that you remembered," said Mrs. Schraalenburgh. "Did anyone else bring a label?"

Sure enough, Cricket was the only one in

the room who had a label. But as she sat glowing with pride at her accomplishment, Zoe Mitchell raised her hand.

"Yes, Zoe?" called Mrs. Schraalenburgh.

"I'll probably have about a hundred labels by next week. Maybe more."

Everyone in the class began laughing.

"That's a lot of soup for you to eat," said Mrs. Schraalenburgh, smiling with amusement.

Someone in the back of the room let out a loud belch at the thought of all that soup.

"I mean it," said Zoe. "You'll see."

Cricket smiled to herself. Boy, that Zoe is really stupid. She couldn't possibly get that many labels in a week. It would take a whole year to eat one hundred cans of soup. Cricket looked across at the new girl. She guessed Zoe wasn't so smart after all. It made Cricket feel a lot better about being in the same class with her.

But during the morning, Zoe proved that she had learned her arithmetic well at her old school. And she was put in the top reading group with Cricket, too.

Cricket worried a bit about lunchtime. Would the girls all start bringing sour pickles in their lunch? She was quite relieved to discover that no one had a pickle today.

"My mother said if I ate a whole pickle I'd get too thirsty," said Hope, explaining why she didn't have one. Cricket was glad that Hope hadn't thought of bringing just a piece of pickle. If all the girls were eating pickle slices, they could still have a pickle club and she would be excluded.

"What kind of sandwich are you eating?" she asked Zoe.

"Mayonnaise and strawberry jam."

Cricket looked at the new girl incredulously. "You're kidding," she insisted. No one could eat a sandwich like that.

"No really," said Zoe. "It's delicious. Do you want a bite?"

Cricket shook her head as Zoe held out her sandwich. None of the other girls sitting around them wanted to try it either.

"I've got peanut butter and strawberry jam," said Connie. "That's good enough for me."

"There's mayonnnaise on my sandwich," said Cricket. "But I think it goes better with tuna than with strawberry jam." She giggled. Everyone else thought Zoe's lunch was crazy, too. Today is turning out much better than yesterday, Cricket thought.

After lunch, the students had art class. They

would have it every Tuesday afternoon. The boys and girls put on the old shirts that they had brought to school. Of course, Cricket noticed with superiority, only about half of the class remembered to bring shirts. She hoped they would get good and messy. It would serve them right.

Cricket looked down at the red corduroy jumper that she was wearing. She certainly didn't want to spill anything on it. But even without an apron or a smock, she knew she was always neat and careful. She knew she wouldn't spill anything.

The first art project, they were told, would be constructing masks out of papier-mâché. First the children were shown slides of masks that had been made by people in Africa and other faraway places. Then they were given newspaper to cut into strips. It was boring. But the next step was more fun. They made a paste of flour and water and pasted strip after strip of newspaper, one on top of the other.

"I'm going to make a Frankenstein mask," said Lucas Cott.

"You already look like Frankenstein," his friend Julio told him.

The girls talked among themselves, too. It was hard to decide what sort of mask to make. The art teacher looked at the clock. "It's time to put your work away," she said. "We will continue the next time you come to the art room."

There was a sink in the art room and the children lined up to wash their hands. There was a roll of paper towels so that you could dry yourself. But most of the boys just wiped their hands on their pants or on their smocks.

When she was back at her desk, Cricket looked down at her hands. They still felt sticky from the art class. There was flour and water paste sticking to her ring, too.

She raised her hand and asked permission to go to the girls' room. When Mrs. Schraalenburgh said that she could go, Cricket took the wooden pass and went down the hall. In the girls' room, she put her hands under the faucet and rubbed them. Some of the paste was stuck under her ring. Carefully, Cricket removed her ring and washed it off. She remembered her mother's warning about losing it, and so instead of resting the ring on the sink, she put it between her teeth. Now she didn't have to worry about her ring getting lost and she could do a better job of washing her hands, too. She was pleased with herself for thinking of such a clever way to keep her ring from getting lost. She wondered why she had never thought of doing it before.

Just then, the door opened with a loud bang and closed with an even louder one. Someone had entered the girls' room. The noise startled Cricket and something terrible happened: She swallowed her ring. For a moment, she stood in front of the sink helplessly. What could she do? She felt a funny pressure in her throat where the ring had rubbed as it went down.

She rushed out of the bathroom and back to her class.

"Cricket, what's wrong?" asked Mrs. Schraalenburgh as she ran into the classroom and up to the teacher's desk.

"I lost my ring," Cricket gasped out. "I swallowed it."

"You did what?" asked the teacher.

"I swallowed my ring." Cricket started to cry.

"Swallowed your ring?"

Lucas Cott jumped out of his seat in the back row and came forward.

"I know what to do," he said. Then, without

waiting for anyone to tell him to do anything, he gave Cricket a hard thump on her back.

"Lucas!" Mrs. Schraalenburgh raised her voice. "What are you doing out of your seat?"

Lucas didn't pay any attention to the teacher. Instead, he gave Cricket two more hard thumps. Cricket didn't know what hurt worse: Lucas hitting her on the back or the funny feeling in her throat. Lucas pounded her back one more time. It was the hardest hit of all. And suddenly, the ring came flying out of Cricket's mouth and landed on the floor.

"See!" Lucas shouted in triumph.

The other students in the class let out a cheer.

"I told you I knew what to do," said Lucas proudly. "My little brother Marcus swallowed a nickel last week. So I'm an expert about things like that."

Cricket picked up her ring and continued crying. She had never done anything so embarrassing before. She had taken off her ring, even though her mother had said to never take it off. And then she had swallowed it, just like a baby. And her throat still hurt, too.

"Zoe. Please take Cricket to get a drink of

water at the fountain," said Mrs. Schraalen-burgh. "I think she will feel better. And please get the wooden pass from the bathroom where she left it."

Cricket followed Zoe out of the classroom.

"It must have been scary to swallow your ring," said Zoe sympathetically. "I'm glad you were able to spit it up."

Cricket bent down at the fountain and took a big gulp of water. Her throat felt scratchy and her face was burning hot from the embarrassment of what had happened. She wished Zoe weren't standing right there watching her every second.

"Do you feel better now?" Zoe asked.

Cricket nodded her head. She did feel a little better, but it was no thanks to Zoe. She wondered what would have happened if Lucas Cott hadn't given her that thump on the back.

The two girls walked down the hallway, and Zoe picked up the wooden pass that was still resting on the edge of the sink in the bathroom where Cricket had left it. Then Cricket followed Zoe back into the classroom. The first day of school had been bad, she thought. But the second day was much worse.

4

"Personality of the Day"

By the time Cricket got home from school, her ring was on her finger and her throat was no longer so scratchy. But still, Cricket felt bad. She didn't know if she should tell her mother what she had done. She always told her mother everything. But she had never done anything like this before. Suppose her mother forbade her to wear her precious ring? Suppose her mother scolded her for almost losing it?

So, for the second day in a row, Cricket didn't say anything about school. She played with her little sister Monica until it was time for her piano lesson.

Monica was almost a year old. She couldn't walk yet, but she loved to crawl on the floor and play with her big sister. Cricket was fascinated by Monica. She wished she could remember how it had felt when she had been that age and size. She was planning to teach Monica everything she knew, so that when Monica went to school she would be the smartest in her class. Cricket had always been the teacher's pet and that's what Monica would be, too.

The only problem was that this year, in fourth grade, no matter how neatly Cricket did her work or how promptly she answered a question, Mrs. Schraalenburgh didn't seem to single her out the way teachers had in the past. Cricket didn't know why, but she had a feeling it was Zoe Mitchell's fault.

At ten to four, Cricket left the house to walk to her piano lesson. She had been taking lessons with Mrs. Aubrey for two years, and she loved playing the piano. But today, when she was playing "Für Elise," she was still so busy thinking about Zoe and what had happened at school that she made several mistakes.

"You will have to practice harder," scolded Mrs. Aubrey.

Cricket's eyes filled with tears at this unexpected criticism from her piano teacher. She *had* practiced a lot, and when she had played the piece at home, she hadn't made a single error. Everything seemed to be going wrong these days. And once again, Cricket wondered if it was because of Zoe Mitchell.

The following Monday, when Zoe came into class carrying a large box, Cricket was certain that something was about to happen to make her feel worse.

Zoe sat down in her seat and immediately raised her hand.

"Yes, Zoe?" called the teacher.

"I brought the soup-can labels that I promised," said Zoe.

"That's lovely," said Mrs. Schraalenburgh.

Cricket pulled out the two labels that she had brought from home. She would have gotten more, but when she phoned her grandmother and asked her if she would save some labels for Cricket, too, her grandmother said she had just sent the labels from all the soup cans in her cupboard to the newspaper. Cricket didn't know why she had to send them *there*.

"Did you get a hundred?" Lucas called out to Zoe.

"I don't have a hundred labels," said Zoe.

"I didn't think you would," said Mrs. Schraalenburgh. "That's a good goal for the entire class. But one hundred labels from a single child would be an impossible feat."

"I have two hundred and seventeen labels," said Zoe, getting up from her desk and presenting the box to Mrs. Schraalenburgh.

The teacher raised the lid from the box to look inside. Sure enough, the box was crammed full of red-and-white soup-can labels.

Everyone in the class started talking at once. How could one family eat that much soup? Cricket looked down at the two labels in her hand. One was for split-pea soup, which she hated. But she had eaten it anyhow. She felt tears coming to her eyes. What was the use of eating split-pea soup if all it accomplished was a single label?

"How in the world did you get so many?" asked Mrs. Schraalenburgh.

"My stepfather is a newspaper reporter. He writes a column in the *Evening Star*. Last week when I told him about getting labels, he wrote about it in the newspaper and people mailed him all these labels. I'll probably be getting more, too," said Zoe, grinning proudly.

"That's not fair," said Cricket angrily. She had no doubt that at least a few of the labels in Zoe's box came from *her* grandmother. Why should Zoe get credit for bringing them to school?

"Cricket, you know better than to call out," Mrs. Schraalenburgh reprimanded. "It was very clever of Zoe to think to ask her stepfather to request the labels in the newspaper. It is a triumph for our class, Zoe. I know these will be a wonderful addition to the labels collected by the rest of the school." The teacher beamed at Zoe. "Take this box down to Mr. Herbertson, the principal. He will be delighted with them."

Zoe took the box of labels and left the room. Cricket thought how nice it would be if Zoe got lost and never returned. But she knew it was too much to hope for.

Later that morning, Mrs. Schraalenburgh revealed a plan for the class. "Each day, starting tomorrow, I am going to select one student to be the 'personality of the day.' "

"I have personality every day," Julio called out.

"So I have noticed," said Mrs. Schraalenburgh. "But this is different. The 'personality of the day' will be line leader when we leave the classroom and will be my monitor whenever I need a special helper. And it will be a different person each day, too."

Cricket didn't like it a bit. In the past, she had always been the line leader and monitor for each of her teachers. And she had held that honored position every day of the school week.

"How will you pick the 'personality of the day'?" asked Hope.

Cricket raised her hand. "You could pick the best person in the class," she suggested hopefully.

"In this class, you are all going to work hard and behave your best," said the teacher smiling. "So everyone is going to have a turn."

Lucas raised his hand. "You could do it in alphabetical order," he said.

Lucas Cott would say that, thought Cricket. His name was right at the front of the alphabet. She'd have to wait ages until they got to the letter *K*.

"I could do it alphabetically," admitted Mrs. Schraalenburgh. "But I think it would be more fun if you didn't know when your turn was coming. And the way to put an element of surprise into our 'personality of the day' is to make a lottery out of it. I am going to put everyone's name on a little slip of paper. Then I'll put all the slips of paper in a bowl on my desk. Every morning I will pull out a slip of paper. The person whose name is on that paper will become our 'personality of the day.'"

Cricket didn't like that plan either. How would she know to wear her best dress when it was her turn if she wouldn't know it was her turn until she got to school? Why did Mrs. Schraalenburgh have to be so different from all other teachers?

Cricket liked it a lot less the next morning when Mrs. Schraalenburgh put her plan into action. She reached into the bowl on her desk and pulled out a slip of paper.

"Zoe Mitchell," she read.

Cricket fumed inwardly. "Zoe's so new she won't even know her way around the building if you send her someplace," she pointed out to the teacher.

"All the rooms are numbered. I think Zoe is smart enough to manage," said Mrs. Schraalenburgh, smiling at the "personality of the day." Then she pinned a button on Zoe's shirt that announced to all the class and all the school what her honor was.

When the fourth-graders marched out in a fire drill later in the morning, Zoe proudly led the way. Cricket was furious. Why should someone so new be in front of the class? At least, Mrs. Schraalenburgh should have picked the name of one of the old-timers such as herself. After the fire drill, Mrs. Schraalenburgh decided that she needed some sheets of colored paper. It was Zoe who went to get them from the art room. Zoe beamed with pride when she returned with the paper. You could see she liked being the "personality of the day." It made Cricket feel really cheated. If she had been in either of the other fourth-grade sections, she just knew she would be the class monitor. Hadn't she always been singled out for such special jobs?

The next day Julio Sanchez was picked for the honor. That was truly ridiculous, Cricket thought. Everybody knew that Julio was the biggest goof-off in the whole school. He shouldn't be allowed out of the room to go on errands. He would probably take an hour just to deliver the attendance sheet to the school office. But Julio surprised Cricket by returning to class in record time. "Anything else you want me to do?" he asked the teacher. He was beaming from ear to ear. It was the first time since he had been in school that he had ever been trusted to do anything out of sight of his teacher.

Cricket was resigned to waiting a long time for her turn to be "personality of the day." There were twenty-two students in her class. Zoe and Julio had had their turns. That left nineteen others to be picked before her. She just knew it was going to take until October before she would have a turn. So she was overjoyed on Thursday morning when Mrs. Schraalenburgh pulled the slip of paper with her name on it out of the bowl.

Cricket was sorry that she was wearing an old faded blue T-shirt and not one of her newer ones. Still, she looked down proudly at the button Mrs. Schraalenburgh pinned to her shirt. "Personality of the day." Perhaps if she was the very best "personality of the day," Mrs. Schraalenburgh would let her have the position every day, after all. She couldn't wait to be given some special jobs to do.

In the morning the class had gym. Cricket proudly led the way out of the fourth-grade classroom. Unfortunately, Mr. Ryan, the gym teacher, made Cricket remove her button. "If the pin comes undone, you could get hurt," he explained. Cricket didn't think it was fair. She was cheated out of wearing the button for a whole period. When Zoe and Julio were "personality of the day," they didn't have to take it off at all.

Mrs. Schraalenburgh didn't have any errands until after lunch. All morning Cricket had been hoping that she would be sent with a message to Mrs. Hockaday, the teacher she had had last year. It was always fun to visit the classroom of the teacher you had the year before. The children in the old teacher's new class always looked like babies. It made Cricket feel extra grown-up to think that she had sat in one of those seats the year before.

Unfortunately, Mrs. Schraalenburgh didn't send Cricket to Mrs. Hockaday. Instead, she gave her a note on a folded sheet of paper and asked her to deliver it to Mrs. Lento, who was one of the other fourth-grade teachers. That was fine with Cricket. She would get a chance to look around the classroom and see some of her former classmates. Maybe they would think she was "personality of the day" every day.

Cricket took the paper from Mrs. Schraalenburgh and walked down the hall. Mrs. Lento's door was open, so Cricket walked right inside. Mrs. Lento was sitting at her desk and speaking to the class. She held out her hand and took the note from Cricket. While the teacher was reading it, Cricket looked around the room. She was looking for clues to see if it would have been better to be in this class instead of the one she was in. One of the girls in the front row smiled at Cricket. It was Melanie Crawford. She had been in second grade with Cricket. That seemed like a hundred years ago.

After she read the note, Mrs. Lento handed it back to Cricket. "All right," she said.

Cricket stood waiting. Maybe Mrs. Lento was going to write a note to Mrs. Schraalenburgh.

"I said all right," Mrs. Lento repeated. "You can go back to your class now."

Some of the children in the room tittered. Cricket felt her face growing red. Wasn't Mrs. Lento going to give her a note for her teacher? As she walked out of the room, it occurred to her that perhaps Mrs. Lento had written her response right onto the note that Cricket had given her. Cricket opened the paper to check. She hoped that Mrs. Lento had written on it because otherwise it might look as if Cricket hadn't really delivered the message.

"Young lady," a voice called out.

Cricket turned her head.

"Young lady, you come back into this classroom at once," the voice shouted.

Cricket turned with relief. It was Mrs. Lento calling her. Obviously, she had realized that she had forgotten to answer the note that Cricket had given her.

"Do you know that what you did is very dishonest?" Mrs. Lento asked Cricket.

Cricket stared at the woman speechlessly. "I didn't do anything," she said.

"You most certainly did. You were reading a piece of mail that was not meant for you. You should be ashamed of yourself."

"I wasn't reading anything," Cricket protested.

"I saw you with my own eyes," said Mrs. Lento. "You were reading this note that Mrs. Schraalenburgh asked you to bring to me."

For a long, long moment, Cricket was so stunned by the unjust accusation that even though she wanted to be a lawyer, she was unable to come up with a single word in self-defense.

"I'm going with you back to your classroom right now. We'll see what Mrs. Schraalenburgh has to say about students who read teachers' mail." Mrs. Lento gestured to a young woman who was sitting in the back of the room. "Please take over until I return," she said.

It must have been a student teacher, Cricket thought numbly as she followed Mrs. Lento out of the door. She could hear all the children in Mrs. Lento's room whispering about her. It was awful.

Mrs. Schraalenburgh looked very surprised to see Cricket accompanied by Mrs. Lento. At least Mrs. Lento didn't announce out loud what had happened. She motioned to Mrs. Schraalenburgh and the three of them stood in the classroom doorway. "This young lady is not worthy of your trust," said Mrs. Lento. "She was standing out in the hallway reading the message that you wrote to me."

"No, I wasn't," said Cricket as tears began to drip down her face. "I only opened the note to be sure you wrote something on it. I didn't want Mrs. Schraalenburgh to think I didn't get an answer from you."

"You still had no business opening it," said Mrs. Lento.

Cricket brushed away her tears. A lawyer wouldn't cry, she thought. She took a deep breath before she spoke. "All I did was glance at the paper to see if there was anything written in another handwriting. I wouldn't read a teacher's messages. And it's just circumstantial evidence for you to accuse me. The note was opened, but I didn't read it. I don't know what it says. You can give me a lie-detector test if you want. Then you will see that I am innocent."

Mrs. Schraalenburgh put her arm around Cricket. "Take it easy," she said softly. "We don't keep lie detectors in this school because we believe our students when they tell us something. If you say you didn't read my message, then I trust you to be telling me the truth.

"Now why don't you go to the girls' room and wash your face before you come back into the class." She turned to Mrs. Lento. "It's all right," she said to her. "I'm sure Cricket didn't mean to do anything wrong. It was just a misunderstanding."

Cricket went and splashed her face with cold water. Even though Mrs. Schraalenburgh had defended her and believed what she said, she still felt bad. It took her a few minutes before she felt she could return to the classroom and not start crying again. Finally, she walked back to her class.

Everyone in the room turned to look at Cricket. She knew they were all curious about what had happened. They would find out soon enough when they talked to their friends in Mrs. Lento's class. But for the moment at least, she could pretend that everything was fine. Mrs. Schraalenburgh called for everyone's attention. She was writing something on the chalkboard that they had to copy. Cricket was glad to have something to keep her and all of her classmates busy. And she was very glad at the end of the afternoon to unpin her button. "Personality of the day" had turned out to be a terrible burden. She was glad it wouldn't be her turn again for a long time.

She thought of how Mrs. Schraalenburgh had put her arm around Cricket's shoulder and said that she trusted her. If Mrs. Schraalenburgh said that, she must mean it. There was only one thing to comfort Cricket as she walked home from school that afternoon. She was glad to be in Mrs. Schraalenburgh's class and not Mrs. Lento's.

5

Cricket
and the
Bee

As the days and the weeks of fourth grade continued, Cricket was more determined than ever to prove to her teacher what a good student she was. It never seemed so difficult before, she thought. But after all, she had never been in fourth grade before either. Probably it would get harder and harder every year that she was in school. Still, she was determined to prove to Mrs. Schraalenburgh that she was a superior student. She worked very hard and raised her hand to answer every question.

When the students were assigned to write

reports about herbs and spices, she deliberately picked a hard one. Thyme. She left the popular ones that everyone had already heard about for the others: pepper, salt, cinnamon, paprika. She went to the library and looked in three books to find as much information as she could.

Cricket's mother helped her, too. Mrs. Kaufman said that the herb was pronounced "time." "The *h* is silent," she explained to her daughter. Cricket tried to remember that as she wrote her report. Her mother let Cricket bring to school the small jar of thyme that was in her spice rack so that the fourth-graders could see and smell the powdered herb.

Cricket had covered two sides of a page with her very neat cursive writing telling all there was to know about thyme. Most of Cricket's class-mates wrote only a paragraph for their reports.

Cricket was very proud when Mrs. Schraa-lenburgh returned her paper with a big red A on it. And she was even prouder when she was asked to read it aloud to the class. Cricket stood in front of the class and began reading. Almost immedi-ately, Zoe's hand was in the air.

"Yes, Zoe?" called the teacher.

"Cricket pronounced it 'thighmme,' but it

really should be 'time.'"

"Good for you, Zoe, for knowing that," said Mrs. Schraalenburgh. Then she explained to everyone about the silent *h*.

Cricket was furious with herself for forgetting. She had been so excited about reading her report aloud that she had forgotten the pronunciation of the word. And as if that wasn't bad enough, Zoe had corrected her.

When Mrs. Schraalenburgh announced that she was going to hold a spelling bee on the first Friday of October, Cricket knew that finally she would have a chance to triumph. Her teachers in the past had always said that she was a natural speller. Not only could she always spell all the words on the class spelling lists, but she could almost always spell new words, too. All week before the first Friday in October, Cricket practiced spelling new words. It was so easy that after a while she made up a game for herself.

"I can spell backwards, too," she announced to the girls sitting near her at lunchtime.

"Let's hear you spell 'Schraalenburgh,' "said Zoe.

Cricket closed her eyes for a moment and then spelled, "H-G-R-U-B-N-E-L-A-A-R-H-C-S."

"Chocolate," said Hope, reading the word off the candy bar that was in her lunch bag.

"E-T-A-L-O-C-O-H-C."

"I bet I could do it, too," said Zoe. "Try me."

"Mississippi," said Cricket. Zoe spelled it backwards without a mistake.

For the rest of the lunch period, the girls tested one another on backwards spelling. Robin Sharolton got so confused she couldn't even spell her own last name in the new backwards way.

By Wednesday Cricket thought she would explode with excitement. She could hardly wait until Friday afternoon.

"Will there be a prize?" Lucas asked.

"You will have to wait and see," the teacher said.

"No fair," Julio called out. "How do I know if I should bother to study or not?"

"Julio, it is not fair to me or to the rest of the class to have you constantly interrupting us with your calling out. I have told you that before and I don't want to have to tell you again. Is that clear?"

"Yes," said Julio. "But I still want to know if there is going to be a prize."

"And you are still going to have to wait and see. To learn how to spell is a reward unto itself."

Cricket decided that probably meant there wasn't a prize. But if she was the winner, she wouldn't need another prize. She just wanted to triumph over Zoe once and for all.

Before it was time to go home, Cricket's head began to hurt. At first she thought the headache had come from concentrating so hard on the backwards spelling at lunchtime. She had clearly been the champion, but it hadn't been easy. And the girls were trying to find harder and harder words to stump her with.

"You look very flushed," said Mrs. Kaufman when Cricket returned home after school.

She put out her hand and felt Cricket's forehead. "I think you have a fever," she said.

"I'm okay," Cricket lied. She couldn't bear to get sick. Last year she had been one of only three students in her class to get a certificate for perfect attendance. If she got sick, she wouldn't get a certificate again this year in June. And worst of all, she might miss the Friday spelling bee. She could not possibly miss the spelling bee.

Mrs. Kaufman went to the bathroom and got the thermometer. She took Cricket's temperature and discovered that it was one hundred and two.

"But I'm feeling fine," Cricket protested as her mother tucked her into bed.

"It may just be a twenty-four-hour virus," said Mrs. Kaufman, trying to comfort her daughter. "You'll probably be fine by the weekend."

"I don't care about the weekend," said Cricket. "I don't want to miss school tomorrow. And on Friday we are having the spelling bee."

Mrs. Kaufman pulled down the shade in Cricket's room. "Rest for a little while," she suggested. "I'll get you an aspirin and some fruit juice."

"I don't want to rest," Cricket protested. But she fell asleep without even eating any supper, which her mother said was proof that she was ill. On Thursday when she woke, her temperature was normal, but her throat was scratchy and her nose was running.

"Your fever is gone," said Mrs. Kaufman, "but I'm still not allowing you to get out of bed. You'll get better a whole lot faster if you just take it easy today."

"But I can go to school tomorrow, can't I?" Cricket begged.

"Schools sure have changed if you want to go that badly," said Mr. Kaufman, coming into Cricket's room to say good-bye before he left for work. "When I was your age, I used to pretend that I was sick just so I could stay home."

"We're having a very important spelling bee tomorrow," Cricket explained. "I just have to go to school to take part in it." She didn't even care any more about not getting a certificate for perfect attendance.

Cricket stayed in bed all day on Thursday. It was nice to have her mother bring her breakfast on a tray. Cricket decided to use this extra time to study more new spelling words. She asked her mother to bring her a dictionary, and she lay in bed propped up with two pillows. There were thousands of words in the dictionary and Cricket learned the meaning and the spelling of quite a few of them. Maybe it wasn't so terrible staying home and being sick the day before the spelling bee, after all.

On Friday morning, Cricket jumped out of bed and started to get dressed. But her mother came into the bedroom, shaking her head. "Cricket," she said, "it's pouring rain outside. It would be very foolish for you to go outside in this weather. You will certainly have a relapse. Besides, you may still be contagious and spread germs to your classmates."

"But I have to be in the spelling bee," Cricket protested loudly.

"You'll be in the next one," said her mother. "I'm sure Mrs. Schraalenburgh will have more than one spelling bee. Maybe she'll even have one every month."

Cricket knew she couldn't wait another whole month to show Mrs. Schraalenburgh how smart she was. If she didn't go to school, Zoe would win. It was bad enough that Zoe brought all those soup labels to school and remembered how to pronounce hard words.

Cricket sat in her bedroom feeling miserable. She couldn't go to school and her mother wouldn't let her play with Monica in case she still had germs. Yesterday, being home and studying the dictionary had been fun. But what was the sense of studying more words if she wasn't going to be in the spelling bee? Cricket reached for a book in the bookcase by her bed. She began turning the pages at random. She had read the book before, so she could skip around in it to her favorite parts. Last year her class had conducted a telephone interview with the author. Cricket remembered that after the interview was completed, Mrs. Hockaday had complimented her for asking the best questions. She turned the pages of the book, but she couldn't concentrate. She kept thinking about the spelling bee she was going to miss.

Suddenly, Cricket had an idea. Why couldn't she participate in the spelling bee over the telephone just the way the class had the interview last year? That way no one would get her germs, but she could still show Mrs. Schraalenburgh what a great speller she was.

She ran to her mother and explained her plan. "Would you call Mrs. Schraalenburgh and ask her?" she begged.

Mrs. Kaufman called the school. And in a very few minutes, the whole thing was arranged. In the afternoon, when it was time for the spelling bee, Mrs. Schraalenburgh would phone Cricket at home. Because there was a microphone attached to the telephone receiver at school, the whole class would hear Cricket's responses when she spelled a word. It was a super plan.

For lunch, Cricket's mother opened a can of chicken-noodle soup. Cricket and Monica both had soup, and Cricket had another label to contribute to the school's collection. Cricket took it without much enthusiasm. Since it was impossible to top Zoe's two hundred and seventeen labels, it hardly seemed worthwhile for her to bother collecting any longer.

Finally, it was one-thirty. Cricket sat by the telephone waiting for it to ring. It was twenty minutes to two before Mrs. Schraalenburgh called.

"Some of the boys are concerned that you might cheat, since no one can see you," the teacher told Cricket.

Cricket knew just who the teacher was referring to. "Tell Lucas that I never cheat," she said. "I don't have to. Cross my heart and hope to die." She put her hand over her heart as she made her vow.

"I know that, too," said the teacher. "But I wanted them to hear you say it. Now we are about to begin."

Cricket listened as the teacher called on the students, one by one. The words were easy. *Deceive.* Cricket remembered the rule: "*i* before *e* except after *c*."

Neighbor.

Julio misspelled that one. He had forgotten the rest of the rule: "*i* before *e* except after *c* or when sounded like *a* as in *neighbor* or *weigh*.

Basil . Cinnamon. Thyme. (Mrs. Schraalenburgh was using words from their reports as well as words from the regular spelling list.)

Dictionary. Cricket smiled to herself. The telephone was sitting on top of a bookcase and right in front of her eyes, she could read the letters off her parents' dictionary. It was a good thing that it wasn't her turn. It would have almost seemed like cheating, except that she already knew how to spell *dictionary.*

By two o'clock, there were only three contestants left in the spelling bee. Lucas, Zoe, and Cricket. The words were getting harder, but still Cricket could spell them with ease.

Constitutional. Responsibility. Administration. Imperfection.

Lucas was given the word *prejudice* . Cricket listened as he tried to spell it. She didn't know that word either. She closed her eyes and tried to imagine it. If Lucas missed, Mrs. Schraalenburgh would call on her next with the same word. Cricket opened her eyes and saw the

dictionary. If she opened it quickly, she could find the word. She knew that it started with *pre*.

"P-R-E-J-E-W-D-I-S-E," Lucas spelled.

"I'm sorry," said the teacher. "That's incorrect."

"Cricket. Can you spell *prejudice*?"

Cricket held out her hand to grab the dictionary. But she remembered her promise not to cheat. If no one saw her, what difference would it make? No one would know. Then she shook her head and lowered her hand. She would just make a guess. She was a natural speller. She would probably get it right, anyhow.

"P-R-E-J-U-D-I-S-E," she spelled.

"I'm sorry, Cricket. That is not correct. If Zoe can spell it, she will be the winner. But if she can't, we will have a three-way tie."

Cricket held her breath. Please, please, let Zoe get it wrong.

"P-R-E-J-U-D-I-C-E," Zoe spelled.

"Correct!" called Mrs. Schraalenburgh. "Zoe, you have won the spelling bee."

There was a loud cheer in the classroom, and Cricket pulled the telephone receiver away from her ear so she didn't have to listen. She felt the tears fill her eyes and then begin to slide down her cheeks. Why could that awful Zoe Mitchell spell *prejudice* if she couldn't? Probably it was on her spelling list in her old school. It just wasn't fair. The only good thing was that no one could see Cricket crying. That was the advantage to losing a spelling bee over the telephone.

Something else happened, however, that was much worse than losing. On Saturday, Cricket's father showed her a small piece at the bottom of the one of the pages in the *Evening Star*. It was part of the column that Zoe's stepfather wrote three times a week. "Sometimes Crickets and bees don't mix as well as they might like," he had written.

> The winner of yesterday's spelling bee in Mrs. Schraalenburgh's fourth-grade class was not Cricket Kaufman, who classmates said had always been the best speller in the class. The new champion in spelling is Zoe Mitchell. Her prize was a small pencil sharpener shaped like a globe.

Of course Cricket was furious. It was bad enough to lose the spelling bee and not to win the prize. Why did it have to be announced in the newspaper for everyone in the world to know?

"I don't think everyone in the world reads this paper," Mr. Kaufman said comfortingly.

"I don't think even half the people in town will read it," her mother said. "This isn't real news. It's a human-interest column and it just tells little local stories to amuse people."

Cricket just knew that if she ever won a spelling bee or did anything else better than Zoe, it wouldn't get into the newspaper. Why should Zoe's stepfather think it was amusing to write good things about Cricket Kaufman? So Cricket was angry at Zoe and at Zoe's stepfather and at herself. If she hadn't been so clever to think of entering the spelling bee over the telephone, Zoe would still have won. But at least Cricket Kaufman wouldn't have been able to lose.

6

The Brunch

In the middle of October, when everyone else was thinking about Halloween, Zoe Mitchell arrived in class carrying a pile of white envelopes. Cricket watched as Zoe went up to Mrs. Schraalenburgh's desk and whispered to her. The teacher said something in return, but Cricket could not hear. All morning, Cricket wondered what secrets Zoe and the teacher had. And finally at lunchtime, she came right out and asked her classmate.

"What's inside all those envelopes you brought to school this morning?"

Zoe smiled. "They're invitations. I wanted to give them out right away, but Mrs. Schraalenburgh said I had to wait till it's time to go home."

"What sort of invitations?" asked Cricket. "Is it your birthday or are you having a Halloween party?"

Zoe shook her head. "My birthday is in February and a Halloween party is for babies. I want to have a more grown-up sort of party. So I'm giving a brunch. It's going to be on the last Sunday of this month and all the girls in our class are invited."

When Zoe said that, Cricket knew that there was an invitation in the pile for her. She was relieved to know that she had been included among the guests, even though she couldn't help disliking Zoe so much. How could she possibly like someone who was as smart as she was? Someone who was always working so hard to be the teacher's pet.

Cricket thought about Zoe's party. She had never been invited to a brunch before and it was just like Zoe to think of doing something so different. Brunch is a meal in the late morning between breakfast and lunchtime. Sometimes on

Sundays, Cricket's mother served brunches. She would make waffles or popovers, and the family would eat them late in the morning and then skip lunch.

When the dismissal bell rang that afternoon, Mrs. Schraalenburgh nodded to Zoe. Looking very important, Zoe took her pile of envelopes out of her desk. She removed the rubber band that held them together and then, as the class filed out of the room, she handed one to each of the girls.

"Thank goodness boys didn't get those envelopes," said Lucas Cott as he looked over Cricket's shoulder. They were standing in the hallway outside the classroom and Cricket was reading the invitation.

It's a party!
Sunday, October 26, 11 A.M.
At the home of Zoe Mitchell.
123 Fourth Street.

"It's a brunch party," Cricket told Lucas.

"One of these days I'm going to have a party just for boys," he said. "It's going to be a lupper or a sunch."

"I never heard of a lupper or a sunch," said

Cricket scornfully.

"It's part lunch and part supper!" shouted Lucas and he charged down the hall.

Cricket caught up with some of the other girls from her class. "Are you going to go to Zoe's party?" she asked.

"Sure," said Connie. "I want to meet her stepfather. Maybe he'll write about me in his newspaper column. Then I'll be famous."

"My parents go to brunch parties sometimes," said Hope. "But I'm never invited. I always have to stay home with my big sister. This time, they'll have to stay home instead!"

So even though she didn't really like Zoe Mitchell, Cricket decided she would attend the brunch party, too. She might not like Zoe, but she knew she would have felt terrible if she hadn't received an invitation like all the other girls. Last year, she hadn't been invited to a single birthday party. She hated it when the girls in her class giggled together at lunchtime, talking about parties or other activities in which she had not been included.

On Sunday morning, October 26, Cricket woke early. She put on her favorite red corduroy jumper and a blouse that was white and had red and blue polka dots on it. Her father said she looked very patriotic in that oufit. Cricket liked it because she thought it made her look pretty.

In the next bedroom, she could hear Monica talking to herself. Monica didn't really talk yet, but she made a lot of sounds and sometimes Cricket was sure she could understand real words among the sounds. Cricket went into Monica's room and tickled her little sister through the slats in the crib. Monica pulled herself up to a standing position.

Cricket wrinkled her nose in distaste. Even though she loved her little sister, sometimes she couldn't stand the smell. She was sure that when she was a baby she never smelled like that. Mrs. Kaufman came into the bedroom.

"You look lovely," she said, smiling at her older daughter.

Cricket beamed in agreement.

"Did you wrap the present for Zoe?"

Cricket had told her mother that she didn't need to bring a present because it wasn't a birthday party. But Mrs. Kaufman had insisted that birthday or not, it was a friendly gesture to bring at least a small gift.

So Cricket had chosen a paperback from the

children's books department at the local bookstore. It was a book that she had wanted to read anyhow, and so Cricket had read it yesterday, being careful not to bend any of the pages or soil the book in any way.

"It's all wrapped," said Cricket.

"You'd better have some juice and a piece of toast or something. They may not serve food right away," said Mrs. Kaufman.

"I'm not hungry," said Cricket, but she obediently drank a glass of orange juice. She was a little worried that they might serve sour pickles at the brunch. But she had already decided that she would just say "No, thank you." No one could make her eat them, and there had to be other things at the party that would taste better.

Zoe lived only a few blocks away. Cricket declined her father's offer to drive her there. She liked walking by herself and wanted to feel important when she went to Zoe's brunch party. Only babies needed to be taken places by their parents.

As she walked along the street, crunching leaves under her feet, Cricket wondered about Zoe's family. She knew that Zoe had a big sister. She wondered what Zoe's stepfather was like.

Maybe he walked around with a pad and a pencil, taking notes about things to write in his newspaper column.

Cricket wondered if he would report on the brunch. She wondered what else Zoe had told her stepfather about her. Zoe always acted friendly toward Cricket at school, but Cricket was sure that it was just an act. If she didn't like Zoe, she was sure that Zoe couldn't really like her.

It was very quiet at 123 Fourth Street. Cricket decided that she must be the first guest to arrive. She rang the bell and waited. No one answered the door and so she rang the bell again. She heard steps and a woman wearing a bathrobe opened the door. For one horrible moment, Cricket thought she had come on the wrong date. She knew this was October 26, but maybe the invitation had been for the last Sunday in November and not October. Or maybe she had come to the wrong address..

"Are . . . are you here for Zoe's party?" asked the woman.

Cricket nodded her head with relief.

"Come in," said the woman. "You're a little early and we're not quite ready for guests yet, I'm afraid."

Cricket looked at her wristwatch. It said exactly two minutes to eleven. Two minutes was early, but not *that* early. She followed the woman past the dining-room table, which was laid out with a tablecloth and place settings and a huge jack-o'-lantern in the middle. (Even though Zoe had said Halloween was for babies.) They went into the kitchen, where Cricket saw Zoe mixing something with an egg beater. She was wearing a big apron over her dress. There were also a man and an older girl in the room, cutting things up.

"One of your friends arrived a bit early," said Zoe's mother.

Cricket glanced down at her watch again. It said exactly eleven o'clock.

"I'm not early," she protested. "I'm the first one here, but everyone else is going to be late. It's eleven o'clock."

The man began laughing. "We didn't think of that, Zoe!" he crowed.

Everyone in the kitchen was laughing except Cricket. She didn't know what the joke was.

"Look at the time," said Zoe, pointing to the kitchen clock on the wall. The small hand was pointing to the ten and the large hand on the twelve.

"But it can't be," said Cricket. Her watch ran on a battery and she had gotten it for her last birthday. It always kept perfect time. How could it be wrong now?

"Last night was the time to set clocks back an hour. In the spring we lose an hour to Daylight Savings Time and in the fall we gain it back again," Zoe's mother explained. "Your parents must have forgotten to change the clocks at your house."

Cricket felt her face turning red with embarrassment. How could her parents have been so careless? It was awful to be the only guest at Zoe's house before they were ready for company. She looked at Zoe's stepfather. She just knew he would write about how stupid she had been about coming early. It would be in the newspaper for everyone to read.

She turned to him angrily. "Anyone can make a mistake, so don't you dare write about this in the paper," she said. "It wasn't nice of you to do it before." There, she had been thinking it and now she had said it.

"Here, this is for you," she said, handing Zoe the wrapped package she had been carrying. Since she had already read it, she wouldn't bother taking it home with her. She turned, looking for the door. She wasn't going to stay at this brunch party and be laughed at any more.

Zoe's mother chuckled. "It looks like this young friend of Zoe's is on to you, Ed." She leaned over and kissed her husband. Then, turning to Cricket, she said, "We all live in fear of finding ourselves in the newspaper."

Cricket didn't think she looked very frightened at all. Zoe's mother probably loved seeing her name in the newspaper all the time.

"Wait a minute," called the older girl, grabbing Cricket by the sleeve of her sweater. "Since you got here so early, you can help us. We'll never be ready in time otherwise. It takes Zoe an hour just to peel a single apple."

"Why are you peeling apples?" asked Cricket.

"We're making fruit salad for the first course," said the girl. "My name is Halley. Who are you?"

"Cricket Kaufman," said Cricket, identifying herself. She thought that Zoe was lucky to have such a nice older sister. If only Monica were this big, they could really have great times together now.

Mrs. Mitchell took Cricket's sweater from

her and gave her an apron to protect her jumper. "Why bother peeling the apples?" asked Cricket. "You can leave the skin on. Then the pieces look prettier and it saves time, too."

"You're right," said Zoe, grinning. "I should have thought of that myself." The girls set to work cutting up apples and slicing bananas. There were also oranges and grapes to add to the fruit salad.

As they were cutting up the fruit, Halley turned to Cricket. "Did it ever occur to you that your last name is Kaufman, but you are not a man. You're a woman?"

"I'm not a woman," said Cricket. "I'm a girl. I won't be ten until January."

"Yes, but your name shouldn't be Kaufman. It should be Cricket Kaufperson."

"Halley is very much into freeing our language of sexist references," said Mr. Mitchell.

"Yes," said Zoe. "She says things like 'personhole cover' and 'humankind' and things like that."

Cricket started to giggle. "Did you tell her that Lisa Benson is in our class? She should change her name to Lisa Ben*person*."

"Or Lisa Ben*daughter*," said Halley.

"Or Lisa Ben*sibling*," Zoe added.

They started thinking of other names and words that should be changed. "Don't waste time, girls, or we'll never manage to be ready for the party in time," said Mrs. Mitchell.

"You mean we won't *woman*age to be ready," said Cricket, and everyone laughed. She was feeling much, much better about being here.

When the Mitchell's kitchen clock said five minutes to eleven and Cricket's watch said five minutes to twelve, the doorbell rang. The guests were beginning to arrive. There was a good smell in the kitchen, which turned out to be two large pies that were in the oven. The pies were not like the fruit pies Cricket's mother sometimes made. They were called "quiche" and the fillings were made of eggs and cheese.

They all had fruit salad and quiche and chocolate brownies and milk. No pickles, thank goodness. Afterward, Zoe brought out a tape recorder that belonged to her stepfather. There was a small microphone to speak into. "Everyone is to say one sentence and we pass it around and around," Zoe instructed. "That way we can make up a story."

"Let's make up a spooky story for Halloween," suggested Hope Dubbin.

"Yes, yes," some of the other girls agreed.

"I'll go first," said Zoe. "I was walking in the graveyard and it was dark and I could hear strange sounds all around me."

She passed the microphone to the next girl. After a couple of giggles, the story continued. It didn't sound like much when they passed the mike around but afterward, when all the pieces were played back, it was a great story.

"Too bad we can't write reports for school this way," said Connie.

When the Mitchell's clock said that it was two and Cricket's wristwatch said that it was three, the party was over.

"Good-bye, good-bye," Zoe called as her guests were leaving. But to Cricket she said, "So long, Cricket Kaufperson. I'll see you tomorrow."

Cricket smiled in return. She wondered if her parents had discovered yet that they had forgotten to turn the clocks in the house back an hour. And she wondered how they would feel about changing their last name. Kaufperson. It was really kind of funny. And the brunch hadn't been so bad, after all. Maybe Zoe Mitchell wasn't so bad either.

7

The
Imperfect/Perfect
Book Report

There was no doubt about it. Zoe Mitchell was just as smart as Cricket Kaufman. Everyone who had known Cricket since she had been the star of the morning kindergarten class, back when she was five years old, agreed. Finally, she had met her match.

In some ways, it made Cricket feel strange not to be the best student in the class. But at the same time, she worked harder than ever and found that she liked school better and better. She was learning so many new things. It was hard to decide if it was because now she was in fourth grade or because she was working not to let Zoe get ahead of her. Lucas Cott was smart, too, but it wasn't the same thing. Maybe it was because he was the smartest boy in the class and she had been the smartest girl. Now, whenever test papers were handed back, Cricket craned her head to see what mark Zoe had gotten. Almost always, the two girls had performed equally well.

Mrs. Schraalenburgh beamed proudly at them both when they each got 100 percent on the fractions test in arithmetic. But she also congratulated Julio for improving his score. When Cricket walked to the back of the room to use the pencil sharpener, she was able to see that Julio had almost as many problems wrong as he had gotten right. Mrs. Schraalenburgh was a funny teacher. She always said she was proud of all her students and to prove it she never singled one person out above the others. Maybe that was why it wasn't quite so bad that Zoe Mitchell was such a good student. If Cricket wasn't the teacher's pet this year, neither was Zoe. No one was. With a different "personality of the day" selected each morning, and students like Julio being congratulated even when they could only answer half the questions, everyone was treated equally.

Still, when Mrs. Schraalenburgh said that once a month everyone had to write a book report, Cricket was delighted. She loved reading and a book report would be fun for her to write. She would do one that was so much better than everyone else's that Mrs. Schraalenburgh would have to admit that she was the very best student in the class. Although Cricket was pleased with the new assignment, there were loud groans from the back of the room.

"Quiet!" Mrs. Schraalenburgh scolded. "If you have something to say, raise your hands and I will call on you." She looked at Lucas, who had made the loudest groan.

"Don't you like to read, Lucas?" asked the teacher.

"Sure," said Lucas. "But I don't like writing book reports."

"A book report is a way of sharing something that you have enjoyed with rest of the class," said Mrs. Schraalenburgh. "It should tell your classmates whether or not they too should read that book."

Lucas did not look convinced. Cricket knew he read a lot of books. She saw him checking them out of the school library when the class had library time. But she also knew he was lazy about doing homework. She, on the other hand, couldn't wait to begin. She would make the best book report that anyone ever did. Then, perhaps finally, Mrs. Schraalenburgh would know what a great student she was.

Cricket had read so many books since the school year had begun that at first she couldn't make up her mind which to use for her report. Finally, she decided to write her report on the book that she had given to Zoe. It was *Dear Mr. Henshaw* by Beverly Clearly. It was too bad she couldn't find a copy of it in the library. But Cricket remembered the story very well, and she thought she could write a report from her memory. Her memory was very good and it had been only a couple of weeks since she had read the book.

Cricket sat down and wrote, covering both sides of a sheet of loose-leaf paper as she told all about the book. Then, very neatly, she copied it over. She used a razor-edged marking pen that she had bought with her allowance last week. The letters came out clear and neat, but near the bottom of the page, she made a mistake. Cricket didn't want to have any crossing-out on her report. So she took a fresh piece of paper and copied her report over again, very slowly this time so that she wouldn't make another error. When she was finished, it looked beautiful. It was the neatest piece of homework that she had ever done.

Then, to enhance the report, she decided to make a special cover for it. She took two sheets of red-colored paper. With her pencil and a ruler, she drew lines across the top of the page. She did it very, very lightly so that afterward she would be able to erase the lines. Then, using the block letters that they had been learning to do in art class, she wrote the title and the author.

Dear Mr. Henshaw, by Beverly Clearly.
Book Report by Cricket Kaufman.

Underneath, she drew a picture of a boy sitting at a desk and writing. People who hadn't read the book might think it was supposed to be a picture of Cricket writing her book report, but if you read the book or at least read Cricket's report about it, you would know that it was supposed to be Leigh Botts, the main character in the story. He was always writing letters to his favorite author, who was named Mr. Henshaw. Cricket colored in the picture with her markers, and she erased the lines from the top of the paper.

Cricket had her own stapler. She used it to staple the top cover and the back cover to the page with her report. When she was finally finished, it was time for bed. She had missed her favorite Thursday evening television program. But she was so proud of her completed book report that she didn't even mind. Wait until Mrs. Schraalenburgh sees my wonderful report, she thought. She knew that the teacher would have to be very impressed with her careful work.

The next morning Cricket proudly handed in her report.

"You didn't tell us we had to make covers," said Connie Alf when she saw Cricket's masterpiece.

"We didn't have to make covers," said Julio. Cricket looked at the paper he was putting on the teacher's desk. Wait until Mrs. Schraalenburgh saw that he had written a report about *Mr. Popper's Penguins*, which she read to them at the beginning of September. It was cheating to write a report about a book that you hadn't even read. Listening didn't count. And besides, everyone in the class already knew about the story. Julio will be in big trouble, Cricket decided.

"I wrote about the book that you gave me," Zoe whispered to Cricket as she put hers in the pile. "It was a great book and it was fun to write about it." She smiled at Cricket. But Cricket did not smile back. It hadn't occurred to her that Zoe would use the same book that she did for her report.

"How long was your report?" Cricket asked her.

"It was all one side and a little bit of the other side of the paper," said Zoe.

Cricket began to feel better. Her report was longer and her report had a fancy cover. Her report had to be a lot better than Zoe's. In fact, having another report on the same book to compare with hers would make Mrs. Schraalenburgh realize all the more how much effort Cricket had put into the assignment. She smiled at Zoe. It was a good thing that they had both written about the same book, after all.

Mrs. Schraalenburgh took all the reports and put them inside her canvas tote bag. "I'll take these home to read over the weekend," she promised. "On Monday, I'll give them back and we'll share them together."

All weekend Cricket glowed inside as she

thought about her wonderful book report. She just knew that her teacher was going to love it. She couldn't wait until they were returned on Monday. Mrs. Schraalenburgh would probably write on the report how fabulous it was.

The reports were not returned to the students until after lunch on Monday. Cricket could hardly sit still as the teacher walked about the room handing them back. She decided that she would try and keep a straight face. It would be hard not to grin from ear to ear when she was reading the teacher's comments. But on the other hand, it would look as if she were showing off when other students such as Julio got bad marks on their reports. She held her breath as Mrs. Schraalenburgh stood at her desk and sorted through the remaining papers in her hand.

"Here's yours, Cricket," said the teacher. She patted Cricket on the back. "I'm sure you'll do better next time, so don't worry too much about your grade."

Cricket couldn't imagine what the teacher was referring to. There was nothing written on the red cover of her report, but when she opened it up, she saw a B − written on the top of the page. Cricket couldn't believe it. How could she possibly have gotten such a low mark? This was an A+ report. It didn't make sense. Then Cricket noticed that on the inside of the back cover, Mrs. Schraalenburgh had written a message.

It is careless of you to misspell the name of the author whom you are writing about. The author of this book spells her last name CLEARY. Also, the award that this book won is called the NEWBERY Medal, not NEWBERRY. If you read your report over, you will see that you said the same thing three different times. It is better to say what you have to once and not bore your readers. I am glad you liked this book and I am sure next time you will write a better report to prove it.

Cricket's eyes blurred with tears. She couldn't believe it. Mrs. Schraalenburgh didn't like her report. So what if she had spelled the author's name wrong? What did it matter? She had never said that spelling was going to count in their book reports.

"I am going to have a few people read their reports out loud to share them with us now," said Mrs. Schraalenburgh. "Let's start with Julio," she said.

Cricket blinked back her tears. If she had

gotten a B −, Julio must have gotten a D.

"I gave Julio an A for his report," the teacher said as Julio walked proudly up to the front of the room.

"Even though Julio wrote about a book that we have already read and talked about in class this year, he has captured the humor of the story and what he has to say about the book will make anyone who hasn't already read it want to read it," she said.

Julio cleared his throat and waited until he had everyone's attention. Then he read his report. It was short, Cricket noted. But he made everyone laugh when he reminded them of one of the funny scenes in the book.

"Suppose you wrote about a book you didn't like," said Connie.

"Why would you bother to do that?" asked Mrs. Schraalenburgh. "If you didn't like the book, you should have stopped reading it and looked for another one."

All the children looked at each other. They had never heard a teacher say that you should stop reading a book.

"Do you know how many books are in the school library?" Mrs. Schraalenburgh asked.

"One hundred," guessed Julio.

Cricket raised her hand. She had once asked the librarian, so she knew the correct answer.

"Many, many more than a hundred," said Mrs. Schraalenburgh.

"Two hundred," someone called out.

"No speaking out," Mrs. Schraalenburgh reminded the students. "Cricket, do you know?" asked the teacher.

"Eight thousand," she said.

There were loud gasps. Eight thousand was a big number.

"That's right," said Mrs. Schraalenburgh. "And don't you think that if there are eight thousand books right here in this school building you could find one that you would like? So why would you waste your time reading a book you don't like?"

"But if we have to make book reports every month from now on, we'll need to find more than *one* book," Lucas pointed out.

"That's right," Connie agreed.

"I suspect that if you gave it a try, you could find many, many books that you will like among the eight thousand books in the school library. And what about the public library? Do you know how many books they have there?"

"Eight thousand," someone guessed.

Mrs. Schraalenburgh shook her head. "The next time you go, ask the children's librarian how many books are in the collection there," she said.

"And next time, Julio will write about a new book. One that he hasn't read or heard read to him before," Mrs. Schraalenburgh added. "Right, Julio?"

Julio grinned at the teacher. "Right," he said. "I want to see if I can make an A every time."

"That's the spirit," said Mrs. Schraalenburgh.

Next she called on Zoe.

Zoe went to the front of the room and began reading. Cricket was surprised to hear her name in the report. Zoe read, "I picked this book because it was given to me by my friend Cricket Kaufman. At first I thought I wouldn't like it because it was all in letters. But before I knew it, I was right in the middle of the story of Leigh Botts and his problems . . ."

Cricket could hardly believe that Zoe considered her to be her friend. Just because she gave her that book it didn't make them friends. That hadn't been her idea. Her mother had insisted that she bring a gift when she went to Zoe's party. And now Zoe had gotten an A writing about it when Cricket had only got a B－. It just didn't seem fair.

Zoe finished reading her report. "How many people want to read that book, now that they have heard about it?" asked Mrs. Schraalenburgh.

Every hand in the class except Cricket's went up.

"Now you know why Zoe got an A on her report. She has done an excellent job of sharing her pleasure with all of us. I notice that Cricket didn't raise her hand. But she doesn't have to read the book. She already did," said the teacher, smiling at Cricket. "And when she gave a copy of it to Zoe as a present, she was sharing her pleasure of the book in still another way."

Cricket could have said that when she bought the book for Zoe, she hadn't even read it yet. But she didn't. She liked what Mrs. Shraalenburgh said about her sharing her pleasure of the book by giving it as a present. It almost made up for the bad mark she got.

Mrs. Schraalenburgh wrote Beverly Cleary's

name on the chalk board so that everyone could copy it and said "Now when you go to the library, you'll know who the author is." Cricket blushed to see the correct spelling on the board. It had really been foolish on her part to write a book report when she didn't have the book right in front of her to copy the author's name. She wouldn't make that mistake again.

A few other students read their book reports, too. Cricket noticed that none of them had made covers for their reports. It had been silly of her to waste her time making a fancy cover if Mrs. Schraalenburgh didn't give her extra credit for it.

"There isn't time to read any more reports," said Mrs. Schraalenburgh after a while. "This was just to get us started. Next month, we will have oral book reports and everyone will have a turn. So start looking for a good book to read. Don't wait until the last minute."

The bell rang for dismissal. Zoe edged over to Cricket. "Thanks again for the book," she said.

Cricket nodded her head. She was relieved that Zoe didn't ask her what grade she had gotten on her report. If the situation had been reversed and Cricket had received an A and Zoe had not read her report aloud, Cricket knew she would have been dying to ask.

"I'll bet we have the same taste in books," said Zoe. "Maybe we could go to the library together after school sometime. You could show me the books you've read and I could show you the ones I've read."

Cricket found herself smiling at Zoe. It sounded as if it might be fun. There had never been another girl in school who liked to read as much as she did. Maybe Zoe was right. Maybe she would be a friend to her.

"Okay," she agreed. And suddenly, it didn't matter so much what grade she had gotten on her report. Next time she would get an A. And if Zoe got one, too, it wouldn't be so terrible. After all, they were the two smartest girls in Mrs. Schraalenburgh's class.

8

The Teacher's Pets

One Monday morning in early December Mrs. Schraalenburgh came into class looking very unhappy. The students did not have to wait long to find out what was troubling her.

"My cat Marmalade disappeared over the weekend," the teacher announced to the class. "I've posted signs on all the streetlights, and I hope someone will find him. If any of you see an orange cat in the area around Willow or Spruce Street, please let me know. It may be Marmalade."

"My grandmother had a cat that got lost," said Hope.

"Did she find it?" asked Julio.

"Nope. It just disappeared."

"It must have been kidnapped," said Julio.

"*Cat*napped," Lucas said, correcting his friend.

"I don't think anyone would want to kidnap Marmalade," said Mrs. Schraalenburgh. "He's just an ordinary cat. But he's lived with me for six years, and so I consider him to be a special part of my family and I miss him."

"I'll tell my stepfather to write about it in the newspaper," offered Zoe. "That way a lot of people will be looking for him, and someone will find him for you for sure."

Cricket glared over at Zoe. That was just like her. She'd get her stepfather to write about Marmalade and when the cat was found—no matter who found the cat—Zoe would get the credit. It made Cricket feel furious. The two girls had never gotten around to going to the library together. And the growing feeling of friendship that Cricket had begun to feel for Zoe disappeared quickly at the thought of Zoe finding Mrs. Schraalenburgh's cat.

All day Cricket kept thinking about Mrs. Schraalenburgh's lost cat. Cricket had never had a pet, but she could imagine how bad her teacher felt at losing Marmalade. She hoped that Mrs. Schraalenburgh would find him, but she didn't want Zoe to get all the credit. In the middle of a page of arithmetic problems using decimals, Cricket got a great idea. After school she would go looking for the cat herself. If she could find the missing Marmalade, then Mrs. Schraalenburgh would finally appreciate her. Cricket decided that she would have to go looking this very afternoon. If she waited until tomorrow, when it was in the newspaper, then the streets would be filled with people searching for Mrs. Schraalenburgh's orange cat.

After making her plan, the rest of the day seemed to drag along. But finally the dismissal bell rang. Cricket rushed home and dropped her backpack in the kitchen. "I can't stay," she told her mother. "I'm going to look for Mrs. Schraalenburgh's cat."

"Where is it?" asked Mrs. Kaufman.

"I don't know, but I'm going to find it," said Cricket.

"Are you dressed warmly enough?" asked Mrs. Kaufman. "It feels as if it's cold enough to snow."

"Don't worry about me," Cricket said, reassuring her mother. She was wearing her winter jacket with a hood, and she had on her woolen hat and matching mittens, too.

Willow Street was not far from where Cricket lived. Cricket lived on Sycamore Street and all the streets near her home were named after other trees. There was Ash and Maple and Elm and Spruce and Willow.

As she got closer to Willow Street, Cricket slowed her pace. She looked around, wondering if any of the other kids in her class had gotten the same idea about looking for the cat. It would be just like Lucas to show up, she thought. Luckily, there was no sign of Lucas and his sidekick Julio or any of her other classmates.

Cricket looked for the missing cat behind every tree and underneath the cars parked on the street. Once she thought she saw a cat jumping out of a pile of raked leaves, but it was only a squirrel. He ran up a tree and was soon being chased by another squirrel. The cold stung Cricket's cheeks and when she exhaled steam came from her mouth. Cricket wondered if the squirrels ever got cold. Maybe the reason they run around so much is so they can keep warm, she thought. A woman came by, walking her dog. "Have you seen an orange cat?" asked Cricket.

"No, I haven't," said the woman. "I don't usually notice cats, but Comet always does. He charges after them and pulls me behind. He hasn't found any cats to chase this afternoon, I'm glad to say."

Cricket passed a streetlight and saw one of the signs that her teacher had posted.

Lost my orange cat, Marmalade.
Reward. Schraalenburgh
17 Willow Street.

Cricket felt someone behind her. She turned to look. Standing there, reading the notice over Cricket's shoulder, was Zoe.

"Hi," said Zoe when Cricket faced her.

"What are you doing here?" asked Cricket indignantly. It hadn't occurred to Cricket that Zoe would have the same idea that she had. Hadn't she said that she would tell her stepfather to write about it in the newspaper? Wasn't that enough for her to do?

"I'm looking for Marmalade," said Zoe smiling. "Just like you."

"I thought your stepfather was going to write

about it in the newspaper," said Cricket.

"I'm going to tell him about it when he comes home tonight. But in the meantime, it's pretty cold. It must be awful for a cat to be lost outside in this kind of weather. It would be much better if we could find him today instead of waiting for people to start looking for him tomorrow."

Cricket was surprised by Zoe's words. Her classmate seemed to be really worried about the cat freezing to death. She hadn't come just to get the credit for finding the cat.

"Maybe we can find him together," suggested Zoe again. "Please, can I look with you? I'm afraid I'm going to get lost. I still don't know my way around here very well. I brought the street map that comes with the telephone book. But I'm not too good at mapping skills. We didn't study that at my old school."

"If you get lost, your mother will have to put a sign up on the other side of these streetlights," said Cricket, giggling.

Zoe giggled, too. "It seems silly when I'm with you. But I was really getting scared," she admitted.

Suddenly, Cricket was no longer annoyed by

Zoe's presence. Zoe had been scared walking these streets by herself. But with Cricket beside her, she wasn't frightened any more. And Cricket, who hadn't felt at all scared walking in this neighborhood, felt that it would be much more fun to have a companion during the search.

"I've been looking underneath cars and behind trees, but I haven't seen any cats," she told Zoe.

"Did you walk down this street yet?" asked Zoe.

"No," said Cricket. "Let's go now."

Together the two girls crossed the street and went to the next block. They saw a black-and-white cat when they crossed the street. The cat was walking slowly, as if deep in thought. "Too bad we can't ask the cat about Marmalade," said Cricket. "I bet he'd know where to look."

"When we get to junior high, we'll get to take another language," said Zoe. "But they never teach us Cat or Dog. That would be more useful."

Cricket laughed. "Even if we don't find Marmalade, this is fun," she said. She was surprised to find that she was having a wonderful time.

"Would you come home from school with me tomorrow?" Zoe asked. "I'll ask my mother to take us to the ice-skating rink. That is, if you'd like to go. Otherwise, we could do something different."

"I have my piano lessons on Tuesday afternoons," Cricket explained. It had been a long time since she had played after school with a friend. She felt a little shy. "Besides, I'm not very good at ice skating. I can't do any tricks or anything."

"I learned how to skate backwards last year," said Zoe. "I could teach you. It isn't hard."

"Only the ice is hard when you fall," said Cricket.

Zoe laughed. "You say funny things," she said. "It's fun to be with you. And don't forget, we said we would go to the public library together, too. There are lots of things we could do together."

The new feeling of warmth that had been kindling inside Cricket was growing bigger by the minute. Zoe really seemed to want to be her friend.

Suddenly, Cricket noticed something underneath a large hedge. Three cats were sitting together. "Look," she said, grabbing Zoe by the arm. "Do you see them?"

"It looks like they are having a meeting or something," Zoe whispered to Cricket.

One of the cats seemed to be the black-and-white one they had seen before. The second cat was gray and orange and black and white. "That's a calico cat." Again Zoe whispered to Cricket.

The third cat was orange.

"That's Marmalade," Cricket whispered excitedly to Zoe. She didn't know why they were whispering. It just seemed right at this crucial moment.

"I'll stay here and you go around the other side," Cricket instructed Zoe. "That way, we'll have Marmalade surrounded."

Cricket was glad that Zoe did as she had asked, without questioning or arguing. Cricket quietly walked toward the cats. She knew that if she moved quickly the cats would be scared, so Cricket took very small steps and paused after each one. The cats did not seem to be paying any attention to her or to Zoe. That was good. Then Zoe stepped on a twig and it broke with a snap. All three cats tensed at once. The calico cat

darted out from the hedge in one direction and the black-and-white one went in another direction. Cricket pounced down on the orange cat and discovered that she had actually succeeded in catching it.

"We've got it!" Zoe shouted. It wasn't fair of her to say "we" when it was Cricket who had caught the cat and Cricket who was struggling to keep it now. But that didn't seem important now at all. The important thing was that orange cat was no longer lost. Cricket was glad that she was wearing her heavy jacket and her mittens because Marmalade was fighting to get free. If all this had happened in warm weather, she would have been scratched to pieces.

"Let's hurry to Mrs. Schraalenburgh's house," she panted. She didn't know if she would be able to make it because the orange cat was struggling so hard to get away. But now that they had found Marmalade, Cricket had no intention of letting him get away. They crossed the street and half-walked, half-ran toward Willow Street.

"Is he heavy?" asked Zoe.

"It's not that he's heavy," said Cricket, panting for breath, "but he won't hold still."

"We're almost there," Zoe encouraged her. "This is number eleven."

They ran down the street, checking the house numbers as they went. The cat began to yowl in protest.

"We're taking you home," Zoe explained. But Marmalade didn't seem to care.

Finally, they reached the door of number seventeen. Zoe pushed the bell. The cat was trying harder than ever to escape Cricket's hold. Cricket wondered if she would have anything left in her arms by the time Mrs. Schraalenburgh came to the door.

When the door opened, Cricket pushed herself inside without saying a word. It was not a moment too soon. The orange cat freed itself from her hold and leaped away. Luckily, he ran farther into Mrs. Schraalenburgh's house instead of out the door.

"We did it," Zoe said triumphantly. "We found Marmalade for you."

Cricket was exhausted. She stood looking around her and trying to catch her breath. She had never been inside a teacher's home before.

"Now my stepfather won't have to write about it in the newspaper, after all," said Zoe.

"That's right," agreed Mrs. Schraalenburgh. "I found my Marmalade. He was waiting beside the door when I came home from school today. But whose cat did you bring me?"

"Didn't we bring you Marmalade?" asked Cricket incredulously.

"No. That's what I'm telling you," said the teacher. "Marmalade came home by himself from wherever he spent the weekend."

Zoe went to look under the sofa where the orange cat that was not Marmalade was hiding. "I think he's too frightened to come out," she said. "We found him on the next block. We were sure he was yours."

Mrs. Schraalenburgh picked up a large orange cat that had just entered the room. "This is my pet," she said. "This is Marmalade."

The real Marmalade was bigger and cleaner and fluffier than the cat that Cricket and Zoe had delivered to the teacher's house. But he wasn't more orange. Cricket and Zoe looked at each other. It was hard to believe they had spent the afternoon looking for a lost cat that wasn't lost. Both girls started laughing at the silliness of the situation at the same moment.

"Perhaps if I offer it some food, this other

cat will decide to come out from under the sofa," said Mrs. Schraalenburgh. She went into the kitchen. Cricket and Zoe stood where they were. Cricket wondered who this other orange cat belonged to. Maybe right now, someone else was putting a sign up on the other side of the streetlight offering a reward for this lost pet.

The cat did not come out right away. It took several minutes for the smell of the cat food to lure him. However, once he did come out he began to gobble up the contents of the dish very quickly.

"The poor thing is starving," said Mrs. Schraalenburgh. "He doesn't have a collar. I'll bet he's a stray."

"What will you do with him?" asked Cricket.

"Poor thing," said Mrs. Schraalenburgh. "He eats as if he hasn't had a meal for weeks." She turned to Marmalade who was sitting on the floor watching the strange cat. "Sweetheart," she said, "don't you think we should adopt this poor fellow? That is, if he really is a stray. But I'm sure he is. Look. He ate the entire dish of food already."

"You mean you're really going to keep it?" asked Zoe.

Mrs. Schraalenburgh smiled and nodded her head in agreement. "I'll post a sign that I found him. If he isn't claimed, he can stay here. Orangeade would be the perfect name for him. Don't you think so?"

Both girls agreed. Mrs. Schraalenburgh took them into her kitchen. She made them wash their hands after handling the stray cat. "Tomorrow, after school, I'll take him to the vet. He probably has never had any shots or anything."

After the girls had washed their hands, Mrs. Schraalenburgh made them each a cup of cocoa and served graham crackers with it.

"You really should give us orangeade to drink," said Cricket.

Zoe giggled.

"You need something warm after traipsing about on such a cold day. You are both dears to have concerned yourselves so much about my cat," Mrs. Schraalenburgh said.

"I guess Marmalade means a lot to you," said Zoe.

"If you've never had a pet, it will seem strange," said the teacher. "But I love Marmalade. And you know, I already feel a bond of affection for poor Orangeade. He looks as if he has led a hard life."

"I don't have a pet, but I have a baby sister," said Cricket. "That's the way I feel about her, too."

Just as the girls finished their cocoa, Mrs. Schraalenburgh's husband returned home from work. He offered to drive the girls home, as it had gotten both late and dark outside.

"Tell me," he asked them as they climbed into the car. "What sort of a teacher is my wife? Is she a good teacher?"

"She's a very good teacher," said Zoe. "She's very fair. In my old school, the teacher always had a pet. Last year it was a girl called Jeanine. Everyone hated her because the teacher favored her all the time. She was so perfect. Even when she wasn't perfect, the teacher acted like she was. Jeanine may have been the teacher's pet, but she didn't have a single friend. Mrs. Schraalenburgh isn't like that. She doesn't have a special pet."

Cricket thought about Zoe's answer to Mr. Schraalenburgh's question. In a way, she had been like that girl Jeanine whom Zoe knew in her old school. When she was the teacher's pet, in the past, she didn't have any friends either. This year she hadn't been singled out as special by the teacher. But she did find that all the students in her class seemed to like her better. Last night Connie had called to ask her to explain the arithmetic homework, and then they had talked together about a program they had both seen on TV. Connie had never called her on the telephone before. And at lunchtime, everyone was friendlier with her than they used to be, too.

"Marmalade is the teacher's real pet," said Cricket.

"And now Orangeade, too," giggled Zoe.

That evening, Zoe telephoned Cricket. She had two questions to ask her. The first was, would she like to go ice skating with her after school on Wednesday. Cricket said yes.

The second question was, could her stepfather please write a story in the newspaper about how they had found the stray orange cat and brought it to Mrs. Schraalenburgh. "He wants to tell about it, but he remembered what you said about using your name in the newspaper. Please say that it's okay," begged Zoe.

Cricket thought for a minute before answering. "Will he write something nice?" she asked. The whole thing had turned out fine in the end, still felt a little silly for bringing the cat into the teacher's home. Would Zoe's father make them sound foolish?

"I promise that it will be nice," said Zoe.

"Okay," said Cricket. "You can tell him yes. He can write about the search for the teacher's pet."

The next morning in school Mrs. Schraalenburgh smiled at both Cricket and Zoe as she reported to the class the good news that Marmalade had returned safely home. But other than that brief announcement, no other mention was made of her afternoon visitors. Cricket realized that she had been silly to expect otherwise. Mrs. Schraalenburgh didn't have favorites. She wouldn't want to single out the two girls who had gone out hunting for the lost cat. She would never be Mrs. Schraalenburgh's special pet. Somehow, knowing this did not make Cricket feel sad today, although a month or two ago, she would have felt awful about it. Instead, she was awfully glad she was in this section of fourth grade. At lunchtime, she sat next to Zoe and they giggled together and planned for their afternoon of skating the next day.

And so on Wednesday two nice things

happened to Cricket. She went ice skating with Zoe. She didn't learn how to skate backwards, but she and Zoe made a date to go skating again on Saturday. In return, Cricket promised Zoe that she would teach her Chinese jump roping. Zoe had never learned how, but it was a popular recess activity in every grade Cricket had ever been in. Cricket had also invited Zoe to come to her house after skating on Saturday. Zoe was going to stay for supper and she would meet Monica, too.

The second nice thing didn't happen until it was almost bedtime on Wednesday evening when Mr. Kaufman was reading the newspaper.

"Cricket," he called. "Come here. I want to show you something."

Cricket came into the living room and looked over her father's shoulder at the paragraph that he was pointing to in the paper. She had forgotten all about the column that Zoe's stepfather wrote for the newspaper.

This is what it said:

On Monday, two fourth-grade students from Mrs. Schraalenburgh's class went looking for their teacher's missing orange cat. Cricket Kaufman and Zoe Mitchell walked up and

n the streets in the cold. In the end they
ound two things. They found the wrong orange
cat and they found each other. Mrs. Schraalenburgh has adopted the homeless stray cat that
the girls delivered to her house. And the girls
have become good friends. Zoe Mitchell said it
was the best thing that could possibly happen
on a Monday afternoon.

Reading the words over her father's shoulder, Cricket Kaufman smiled with pleasure. She
rushed to the telephone to call Zoe. It was the
best thing that could possibly happen on a
Wednesday evening, too.